SPIKE IN THE CITY

written and illustrated by

Paulette Bogan

G. P. Putnam's Sons　New York

Library of Congress Cataloging-in Publication Data
Bogan, Paulette. Spike in the city/ written and illustrated by Paulette Bogan. p. cm.
Summary: On Spike's first trip to the big city he rides in an elevator,
catches a frisbee, and gets lost. [1.Dogs Fiction. 2. Lost and found
possessions Fiction. 3. City and town life Fiction.] I. Title.
PZ7.B6357835St 2000 [E]—dc21 99-31108
CIP ISBN 0-399-23442-x
1 3 5 7 9 10 8 6 4 2
First Impression

With love to

Sharon & Tony
&
My Three Angels,
Sophia, Rachael, & Lucille

Shannon was taking Spike on his first trip to the big city.

First they rode up in an elevator. "AARRROOO!"
howled Spike. Someone kept stepping on his tail!

When they got to the top, Shannon let Spike go
outside. He was up in the clouds with the pigeons!
"YEEOWZZA!" yelped Spike. He did not feel so good.

The city streets were full of new smells.
Spike pulled hard on his leash.

"Do not get lost, Spike," Shannon said.
"Stick by me."

Spike said, "WOOF!" to his first city dog.
But the dog pretended not to hear.

At the deli, Shannon left Spike tied to a parking meter. "I will be back in a minute," she said. But Spike thought they were going to stick together.

A big truck drove by. *Splash!* Suddenly Spike was not a black-and-white dog anymore.

He was a mud-color dog! "GRRRRR," growled Spike,
shaking himself off.

Spike was not sure he liked the city.

At the park Shannon let him off the leash.
Suddenly something whizzed through the air.
Spike caught it! "AARRRFFF!"

When Spike looked up, two dogs were waiting
for their frisbee. They smiled at him.
Hmmmm, thought Spike.

The dogs showed Spike a cat on a leash.
The cat did not say hello. Humpf! thought Spike.

They showed him a man on wheels.
The man was very fast.

But when a dog on a skateboard zoomed by,

Spike wanted to try it for himself. He chased it . . .

. . . under a lot of feet . . .

. . . through the middle of a million dogs . . .

. . . right by a snake with legs . . .

. . . and into a fountain full of pigeons!
"AARRGGHH!" gurgled Spike.

When Spike climbed out, the dog on the skateboard
was gone. He did not see the cat on the leash,
or the man on wheels, or his new friends.

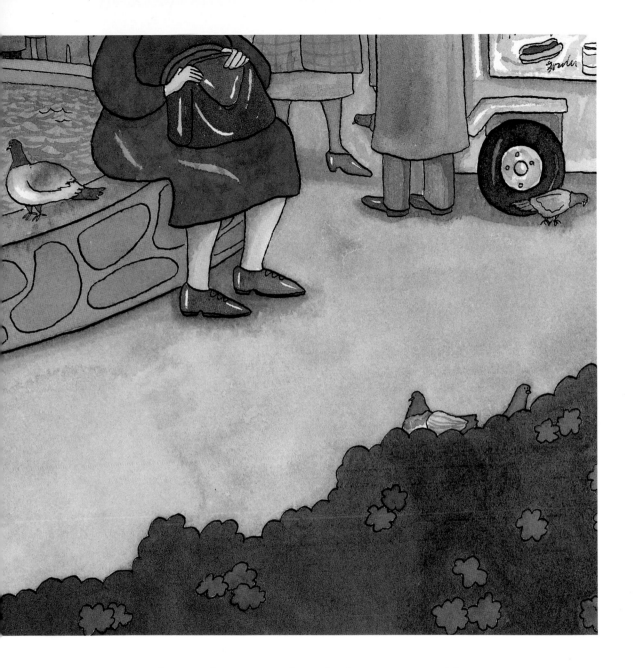

Worse than that, Spike did not see Shannon!
"AAARROOOO!" he howled.

Spike was all alone. He did not know what to do.
He did not know how to get home. Spike sniffed
the air. He sniffed again.

He walked back around the fountain, all through the park, and back to where he started. But this time, no one was there . . .

. . . except Shannon! "I'm so glad I found you!"
said Shannon.

"RRRUFFF!" barked Spike. *Me too!*